FIRE STORM

OUTDOOR ADVENTURES

Jean Craighead George

Wendell Minor

KATHERINE TEGEN BOOKS

An Imprint of HarperCollins*Publishers*

Axel took a flying leap off a riverside boulder. He hugged his knees and cannonballed into a crystal pool in the wild mountain river.

"Come on in, Grits," he called to his little dog. "The water's freezing."

Grits barked and stayed where he was. Axel splashed out of the water and dried himself.

"Get dressed," Aunt Charlotte said to him. "It's getting late, and we haven't found a campsite. Take the kayak and follow us." She and Axel's Uncle Paul pushed off in the big inflated raft and rowed into the swiftest stream of current.

Uncle Paul was a forester. Last winter he had promised Axel that if he got an A in history, Axel's least-favorite subject, he would take him down the treacherous waters of the Middle Fork of Idaho's Salmon River. Axel got the A.

The drudgery had been worth it. Shooting the cascades and the waterfalls was living. He had only dumped twice.

He followed the raft down a cascade, around two boulders, and into calm water. He looked up. A plume of black smoke was towering up from a distant mountain.

It was the summer of 2000, the driest summer in a hundred years. Fires were burning out of control all over the west.

"You won't have a fire problem," the fire warden had said when they started their float trip. "The fires are hundreds of miles from the Middle Fork."

For three days they had paddled in wild beauty. They had seen no cars, no roads, no telephone wires. Eagles, Rocky Mountain sheep, bears, and moose had been their companions.

Aunt Charlotte and Uncle Paul rowed to a boiling waterfall, then sped down it and into another calm eddy. Axel followed with his paddle held high. He let the current steer him right to them. They were staring at the smoke plume. "No threat," said Uncle Paul. "That fire is on the other side of the mountain."

Suddenly a bolt of dry lightning streaked from cloud to ground and hit the ridge above the river. No rain accompanied the strike. The tinder-dry pine needles exploded into flames. The flames raced up the trees.

"That's no Boy Scout campfire," Axel said to Grits, and kept close to the raft. An hour passed.

More dry lightning strikes started new fires. The mountain to the right of the rafting party crackled and roared. Smoke filled the river canyon.

Axel found his way by staying close to shore. When a wind cleared the air, he hurried to catch up with Aunt Charlotte and Uncle Paul. They were beached at White Sand campground, staring up at the flames. They were not setting up camp.

"We should get out of here," Uncle Paul said when Axel jumped from the kayak, "but it's risky. It's too smoky to see rocks and waterfalls downriver. They are dangerous even in broad daylight."

"Let's stay here," Axel said. "The fire's not burning on this side of the river."

"And it won't," said Uncle Paul. "There are too few trees on these rugged cliffs to fuel it." But Uncle Paul did not unpack the camping gear. He kept watching the fires.

Suddenly the wind changed. With a roar, the many fires hurricaned into one thundering fire storm. An orange wall of flame sped down the slope, jumped the river, and fired up the sage and trees behind the campsite.

As Axel and his family stood there, sand, sky, and river shone yellow-orange. Trees exploded like rifle shots. Burning sagebrush spiraled up into the fire storm and turned to dust. Grits whined.

"Let's go," Aunt Charlotte said.

"Wait," warned Uncle Paul. "It's better to sit still in the known than plunge into the unknown. A solution will present itself."

The three sat and waited for a solution. The sun set but darkness did not fall. The sky grew brighter, the air smokier. Aunt Charlotte dipped four bandanas in the river and handed them to Axel and Uncle Paul to tie over their noses and mouths.

Axel tied one on Grits and put him in the bottom of the kayak, where the air was fresher.

They waited. Flaming trees were sucked skyward by the winds that were created by the terrible heat. Black clouds mushroomed and billowed. Breathing became difficult.

Then the fire storm surrounded them. Axel saw no solution anywhere—except, perhaps, in the middle of the river. He located a deep pool where he thought he could survive. That thought calmed him.

Axel waded out into the water.

He leaned down and peered under the smoke.

"Does fire burn in the same place twice?" he called.

"No," Aunt Charlotte answered.

"I see a burned-out campsite not too far downriver."

"Good solution," said Uncle Paul. "Let's go for it." He and Aunt Charlotte jumped into the raft and quickly rowed out into the current. Axel and Grits followed in the kayak.

They pulled ashore at the blackened campsite. The trees and stumps were still smoldering, and the air was thick with smoke, but the fire had passed.

Uncle Paul tossed bailing buckets to Axel and Aunt Charlotte.

"Dump water on the smoldering tree stumps," he said. "We'll spend the night here."

When the last ember was out, they unrolled their sleeping bags and lay down, but Axel could not sleep.

The fire storm was noisy. Trees and even rocks exploded with loud booms. The towers of flames on the ridges whistled and screamed. Burning logs roared down the mountain and rolled to the edge of their campsite, where they slowly went out. There was nothing more to burn.

Looking back through a forest of black sticks that had once been green trees, Axel made out the White Sand campground. It was an inferno of flames.

The next morning the sun shone through dense smoke and colored the river, the boats, and the people a strange fluorescent orange. It was cold. Bandanas over their faces, their eyes watering, the little party cheered when the sun climbed higher. The air cleared, and they could see the river. They pushed off into the charred wilderness.

As Axel passed miles of smoldering trees and smoking stumps, he grew terribly sad. He paddled up to Uncle Paul and Aunt Charlotte's raft and clung to it.

"I can't look any longer," Axel said. "I want to cry for the lost forest."

"It's not lost," said Uncle Paul. "Just altered. It will come back and be healthier."

"No way!" said Axel.

"It's true," agreed Aunt Charlotte. "The forest is a phoenix, like that bird of legend. The phoenix burned itself to ashes and arose from those ashes to live again. The forest will, too."

"Tell me about it," Axel scoffed.

"A blade of grass will appear in the nutrient-rich ashes," she said. "Great swathes of fireweed will grow and blossom. Then a carpet of green shrubs will emerge from old roots. In the snowmelt of spring, little pine trees will push up."

"When I'm an old man," Axel grumbled.

"When we come back next summer," Uncle Paul said.

"That I want to see," said Axel skeptically. "It's a date."

After ten hours of hard paddling, the weary party pulled up at the Cache Creek takeout point.

A tired and discouraged Axel glanced up at the sky. A bald eagle, like the phoenix of legend, soared toward the ruins of the fire.

"I'll see you next summer," he said, and smiled.

AUTHOR'S NOTE

In the summer of 2000, Derek Craighead and his family were rafting the North Fork of the Salmon River in Idaho when a wildfire roared down around them. Unafraid, fascinated, children and adults alike watched this drama of nature with great respect. When they got home, their stories were so galvanizing that I put my adventurer, Axel, in the heart of their *Fire Storm* adventure. The model for Axel is also a member of my family, Scotty Craighead.

—J. C. G.

To Sophie and Derek with love and thanks—J.C.G.

To the Tegen family, especially Tyler—W.G.M.

Fire Storm   Text copyright © 2003 by Julie Productions Inc.   Illustrations copyright © 2003 by Wendell Minor
Printed in the U.S.A. All rights reserved.
www.harperchildrens.com
Library of Congress Cataloging-in-Publication Data
George, Jean Craighead, date
Fire storm / Jean Craighead George ; illustrated by Wendell Minor.
p.   cm.
Summary: Axel enjoys kayaking behind the raft of his aunt and uncle as they journey down Idaho's
Salmon River, until they find themselves in the middle of a forest fire.
ISBN 0-06-000263-8 — ISBN 0-06-000264-6 (lib. bdg.)
[1. Forest fires—Fiction.   2. Rafts—Fiction.   3. Kayaking—Fiction.   4. Idaho—Fiction.]
I. Minor, Wendell, ill.   II. Title.
PZ7.G2933 Fk   2003   [E]—dc21   2002001468   CIP   AC
Typography by Wendell Minor and Al Cetta   1 2 3 4 5 6 7 8 9 10   ❖   First Edition